OTHER YEARLING BOOKS YOU WILL ENJOY
by Patricia Reilly Giff
illustrated by Blanche Sims

THE NEW KIDS AT THE POLK STREET SCHOOL BOOKS:

WATCH OUT! MAN-EATING SNAKE
FANCY FEET
B-E-S-T FRIENDS
ALL ABOUT STACY
SPECTACULAR STONE SOUP
STACY SAYS GOOD-BYE

THE KIDS OF THE POLK STREET SCHOOL BOOKS:

LAZY LIONS, LUCKY LAMBS
SNAGGLE DOODLES
PURPLE CLIMBING DAYS
SAY "CHEESE"
SUNNY-SIDE UP
PICKLE PUSS *and more!*

YEARLING BOOKS/YOUNG YEARLINGS/YEARLING CLASSICS are designed especially to entertain and enlighten young people. Patricia Reilly Giff, consultant to this series, received the bachelor's degree from Marymount College. She holds the master's degree in history from St. John's University, and a Professional Diploma in Reading from Hofstra University. She was a teacher and reading consultant for many years, and is the author of numerous books for young readers.

For a complete listing of all Yearling titles, write to
Dell Readers Service, P.O. Box 1045,
South Holland, IL 60473.

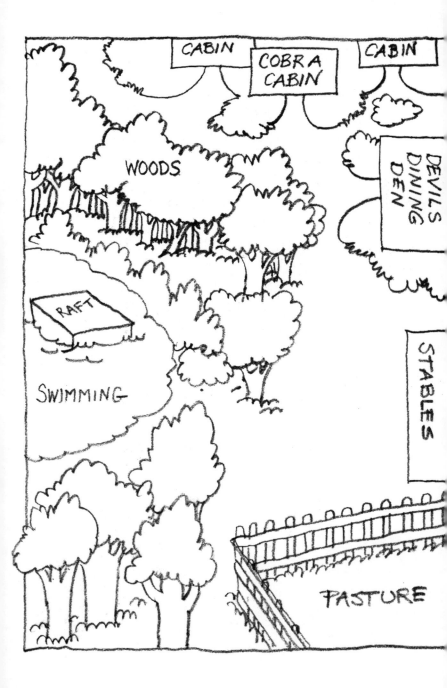

THE POLKA DOT
PRIVATE EYE

GARBAGE JUICE FOR BREAKFAST

Patricia Reilly Giff

Illustrated by Blanche Sims

A YOUNG YEARLING BOOK

Published by
Dell Publishing
a division of
Bantam Doubleday Dell Publishing Group, Inc.
666 Fifth Avenue
New York, New York 10103

ISBN: 0-440-40207-7

Printed in the United States of America

August 1989

10 9 8 7 6 5 4 3 2 1
W

To my dear old Kevin Rooney
of St. Albans,
who taught me basketball
and science.
Love wherever you are.

GARBAGE JUICE
FOR BREAKFAST

···CHAPTER ONE···

Dawn Bosco put on her ladybug earrings.

She reached for her shirt with the lace collar.

Today was a special day in Camp Wild-In-The-Woods.

"Horseback-riding day," Miss Perry called. "Hurry."

Dawn rushed out of Cobra Cabin.

She had to get the best horse.

Jill Simon and Lizzie Lee rushed out too. So did the rest of the campers.

They didn't go straight to the barn, though.

1

Miss Perry pointed. "Sit here under the flagpole," she said. "I have some important news."

"What about the horses?" asked Glenda with the gold fingernails.

"First things first," said Miss Perry.

Dawn sat down.

She wished she had a huge Western hat like Jill Simon's.

She wished she had a cowboy string tie like Lizzie Lee's.

She wished she had a mystery to solve.

"Giddyap," said Lizzie Lee. "Let's get going here."

Everybody laughed. Even Miss Perry.

Miss Perry had a pile of papers in her hand. She waved them around. "Just to give you something to think about . . . I've set up a mystery."

Dawn sat up straight.

Wonderful.

She'd solve it in no time.

She was the Polka Dot Private Eye.

Miss Perry was passing out the papers.

Dawn looked at the top of hers:

HELP US FIND TREASURE

She stared at it.

Treasure!

This might be her best case yet.

Lizzie Lee's hand was up in the air. "Do we get to keep the treasure?"

"Good question," said Gina and Jill Simon at once.

"Very good question," said Dawn.

"No," said Miss Perry. "It's just for fun." She smiled. "Why don't you read the paper?"

Dawn took a peek at Jill.

Jill's Western hat was down over her eyes. Her mouth was open. She was sounding out the words. "Re-re-wwwwwww . . ."

Jill wasn't such a hot reader.

She'd never solve the mystery anyway.

She was a terrible detective.

Dawn looked at Lizzie Lee out of the corner of her eye.

Lizzie was sounding out the words too.

Great!

She'd never get the mystery solved either.

Dawn started to read:

Start at the barn.
Ride a hard horse.
Look up in the air
for the first clue, of course.

Take the right trail,
Turn at the tree.
Be sure it's the one
for Donald and me.

She turned the page over.

There were more clues. At the bottom it was signed D. Perry.

Dawn looked up at the sky.

This wasn't going to be easy.

She began to read again.

Fast.

Then she raced back into Cobra Cabin.

She pulled out her Polka Dot detective box.

She slapped her Polka Dot Private Eye hat on her head.

She was ready to begin.

··· CHAPTER TWO ···

Miss Perry blew her whistle. "Come back," she told everyone. "You forgot something."

What could it be? Dawn wondered.

"Breakfast," said Jill Simon. "I didn't forget. Not for one second."

Everybody laughed.

Everyone except Dawn.

She didn't want to waste time eating.

She wanted to get right to the mystery.

Everyone marched toward the Devil's Den Dining Room.

7

Nellie with the thousand freckles walked next to Dawn. "Shredded wheat for breakfast," she said.

"Are you sure?" Dawn asked. She knew Nellie was right, though. Nellie knew all about camp. She went every single year.

"Yep," said Nellie.

"Yuck-o," said Dawn.

"Hey." Nellie pointed. "Who's that going up the hill?"

Dawn shaded her eyes.

It was Lizzie Lee.

She was climbing as fast as she could.

She was wearing something on her head.

It looked like fur.

A black tail hung down over her ear.

Then Dawn remembered.

Lizzie was the Cool Cat Detective.

Dawn clicked her teeth. That Lizzie. She was trying to solve the mystery first.

8

"Hey, Lizzie. Where are you going?" Nellie yelled.

Miss Perry blew her whistle. "Come back," she called. "It's time for. . ."

Lizzie stopped, one foot in the air. "I'm trying to solve the mystery."

"Shredded wheat," called Nellie, "and garbage juice for breakfast."

Lizzie took another step. "I hate that garbage juice. It has prunes and stuff in it."

Miss Perry laughed. "Me too." She opened the door to the dining room. "It helps your brains grow, I guess."

A minute later Lizzie banged into a seat next to Dawn.

She took a gulp of juice. Then she sucked in her cheeks and squinched her eyes shut.

Dawn shivered. Horrible. She began her cereal.

She'd save the juice for last.

9

Next to her, Glenda wiggled her gold fingernails. "Who do you think will solve the mystery?"

Dawn wiped her juice mustache. "Me."

Lizzie shook her head. "No, me."

Jill pushed her hat out of her eyes. "Dawn's the greatest."

"I think Lizzie," Nellie said.

"Contest," said someone else.

Dawn and Lizzie looked at each other. "This is it," said Lizzie.

"Right," said Dawn. "We'll find out who's the greatest detective."

"Cool Cat," said Nellie.

"Polka Dot," said Jill.

Dawn pulled her treasure paper out of her pocket.

She took a quick look.

Ride a hard horse.

Something with horses, she thought. Something at the barn.

It was a good thing they were going to ride this morning.

She had to solve the mystery before Lizzie Lee.

She closed her eyes and drank her garbage juice.

She stuck a huge spoonful of shredded wheat in her mouth and chewed.

Then she stood up and headed for the barn.

···CHAPTER THREE···

Everyone else was rushing for the barn too.
Dawn slid in first.

Right behind her came Lizzie Lee. Then
Jill, and Nellie, and the others.

Inside it smelled like hay.

It smelled like horses too.

"Easy now," Tex told them. He was wearing a Western hat like Jill's.

It didn't fall down over his eyes as hers
did, though.

Dawn looked at the horses. She read their
names over their stalls.

13

Star. Trixie. Raider. Flash.

Flash's eyes were closed. He was falling asleep.

Dawn spotted a big black horse.

He flicked one ear at her.

Dawn swallowed. He was a lot bigger up close than she had thought.

So were the rest of the horses.

Too big.

"You can pat Blackie's nose," said Tex.

Dawn reached up slowly.

The horse opened its mouth.

It showed about a hundred huge yellow teeth.

It made a sound in back of its throat.

Dawn pulled her hand away.

Everybody laughed.

Lizzie hooked her fingers in her jeans belt. "I'll take that one," she said.

Tex shook his head. "Everyone gets Woodie today."

14

"I don't see Woodie," said Dawn.

Nellie started to laugh. "Woodie isn't a horse."

Tex pointed. A saddle was tied onto a railing. "That's old Woodie."

Dawn nodded. She was glad she didn't have to ride a real horse today.

"Time to try it out," said Tex. "Get up on the left side. A horse may kick if you get up on the right."

Dawn swallowed. She looked at Blackie's hooves.

They looked strong.

The horse looked back at her.

Its eyes were big . . . and not too friendly.

"Let me up first," Nellie said. "I've been here before. I know how to do it."

"Me second," said Lizzie and Jill at the same time.

"I'll be last," said Dawn.

Nellie began to ride. She held the reins.

15

She bounced up and down on the saddle. "Ride 'em, cowboy," she yelled.

"That's it," said Tex. "Nice and easy."

Then it was Jill's turn.

Jill's hat was down over her eyes.

Her cheeks were red.

Her braids bounced up and down.

"I'm not afraid," she said. She sounded surprised.

"Next," said Tex. He pointed to Dawn.

"Go ahead," Lizzie said.

Dawn climbed up. The railing was high. Much higher than it looked.

She closed her eyes for a second.

She held on to the knob in front of the saddle.

"That's the pommel," Tex said. "It's also called the horn."

"Giddyap," Dawn said. Her mouth felt dry.

She tried to bounce a little.

She was up too high, though.

At last Tex said, "Time's up."

It was Lizzie's turn.

Dawn took a deep breath. She was glad to be down on the ground.

She hoped no one knew she was afraid.

She pulled her treasure paper out of her pocket.

Take the right trail,

Maybe she should find the right trail now. Skip the hard horse for a while.

Do it now while Lizzie was up on Woodie.

She looked around.

Everyone was watching Lizzie.

Even the horses.

Dawn backed out of the barn.

Miss Perry was sitting under the flagpole. She was drinking her coffee.

Dawn ducked around the other side of the barn.

Where to begin?

There were a couple of trails.

Too bad she didn't know her right from her left.

She tried to think of the hand she wrote with.

That was her right hand.

She wrote her name in the air, first with one hand. Then with the other.

It didn't seem to work. She still couldn't remember.

She took a breath.

One trail went up the hill. It said East Way.

The other went down. That one said Rolling On.

The down one looked easier.

That was the one she picked.

···CHAPTER FOUR···

Dawn started down the path.

It was cool under the trees. Green.

She could hear birds chirping.

Crickets too.

In the barn Lizzie was yelling, "Ride 'em, cowboy."

Dawn could hear everyone laughing.

She began to run.

After a few minutes she couldn't hear the campers.

A bird was singing over her head, though.

And crickets were chirping all over the place.

She saw evergreen trees now, and huge dark bushes.

The path twisted and turned.

Suddenly it stopped.

In front of her was a tall tree.

A butterfly rested on the trunk.

Dawn leaned forward. She stared at its powdery orange wings.

She could hear something else now.

Mosquitoes.

Yucks.

She'd better get out of here.

She looked around. There was nothing much here anyway.

Yes, a path on the other side of the tree. Mosquito Heaven, said the sign.

She wondered what time it was. Maybe she should go back now.

She frowned. A good detective always searches out the clues.

She had to search the path.

Slap. Another mosquito.

She inched her way around the tree.

She walked a little farther.

Then there were more paths.

One, two, three, four. There were names on all of them.

Dawn scratched her knee.

She could take one of the paths. Take it quickly.

She tried to choose.

Mouse House.

Duck Pond Trail.

Meadow Walk.

Stone Trail.

Then she stopped. It was getting late.

She'd have to wait until there was more time.

She turned and started back.

It was a good thing the butterfly tree was in front of her.

Everything else looked strange. Different.

She reached the tree.

She walked around it.

The butterfly had flown away.

She stepped back. Maybe it wasn't even the same tree. How could she tell?

She might be lost.

She started to run.

A moment later she was back to the four paths.

She was getting hot now, and tired.

Mosquitoes were buzzing all over the place.

She heard something.

It was a soft sound—so soft she almost missed it.

Something rustled in the trees.

She could see the leaves moving.

Everything else was quiet—even the mosquitoes.

She moved away from the sound as fast as she could.

In front of her again was a tall tree.

She raced around it.

Something rammed into her.

"Oooff."

For a moment she couldn't catch her breath.

Then she started to scream.

Someone else was screaming too.

Dawn brushed her hair out of her eyes. "Lizzie Lee," she said.

Lizzie looked scared. She looked as if she were crying.

"Are you afraid?" Dawn asked.

"I'm not afraid of anything," said Lizzie. "I'm a detective." She took a breath. "And stop following me."

"I certainly am not following you . . ."
Dawn began. Then she stopped.

She had just thought of something.

Something important.

It had to do with a horse.

A hard horse.

She raced for the barn.

···CHAPTER FIVE···

It was almost bedtime. Lizzie Lee wiped the window with her hand. "It's raining out," she said.

"It's pouring," said Jill Simon.

Dawn sank down on her bed.

She was glad it was raining.

If it rained tomorrow, she wouldn't have to get up on one of those horses.

She thought about their big teeth . . . their sharp hooves.

She thought about how high up they were.

She sighed. It was cozy in Cobra Cabin.

29

She thought back to her first day at camp.

She had hated it.

The walls were plain wood. Nails stuck out all over. The bunks took up most of the space. And there was only an old skinny-minny black and white TV.

Dawn loved it now, though.

Posters were tacked up on the walls. So were stickers—hearts, and butterflies, and rainbows.

A big rocking chair sat at one end. It was covered with a Mickey Mouse blanket.

"It's my place to think," Miss Perry always said.

Dawn's bunk was her place to think.

She was going to think about the treasure.

She had solved the first clue.

At least she thought she had.

If only she had been able to get back into

the barn today. Then she would have known for sure.

But Miss Perry had called everyone. "Time for a swim," she had said.

Now Dawn sat back in her bunk. She looked at her treasure paper.

> *Start at the barn.*
> *Ride a hard horse.*
> *Look up in the air*
> *for the first clue, of course.*

It was easy. "Simple," she said aloud.

Jill leaned over the bunk. "What's easy?"

"Lights out in ten minutes," Miss Perry called. "Something special first."

Dawn looked up. Something special. She wondered what it was.

Miss Perry was walking from bed to bed.

She was wearing gray sweats.

On front there was a picture of Donald Duck. Underneath it said:

I QUACK
FOR YOU

Miss Perry stopped at Dawn's bunk.

She held out a box. "Something for the Polka Dot Private Eye," she said.

The box was filled with cookies.

They looked like chocolate pretzels.

They made Dawn's mouth water.

"How's the mystery going?" Miss Perry asked. She helped herself to a cookie.

Jill stuck her head over the top bunk. She was still wearing her Western hat. "Terrible. I can't even read the whole thing."

"Keep working on it," said Miss Perry.

Lizzie Lee poked her head out of the next bunk. "What's the reward, anyway?"

Miss Perry grinned at them. "I wondered when someone would ask. It's a party in honor of the winner. And the winner gets to—" She clapped her hand over her mouth. "Can't tell. It has to do with the treasure."

She winked. "You may even get extra garbage juice for breakfast." She waved and turned out the lights.

"Dawn?" Jill leaned over the side of the bed.

Dawn could just about see her head in the dark.

"What's easy?" Jill asked.

"What?" Then Dawn remembered. "The clue. The first clue. The hard horse."

"I bet it's that black one," said Jill.

Dawn shook her head. "No, it's Woodie. A hard horse. A wooden horse. Tomorrow we'll look up. I'll bet we'll spot the arrow."

"Hey, that's right," someone said.

It wasn't Jill.

"Is that you, Lizzie?" Dawn asked.

Lizzie didn't answer.

Dawn gave her pillow a punch.

She had just given a clue away to Lizzie Lee.

···CHAPTER SIX···

Something was after her.

Something big.

It had huge teeth.

Dawn sat up in bed. It's only a dream, she told herself. A dream about a horse.

She opened her eyes.

It was dark.

Something was banging over her head.

What was it?

"Rain," said Jill Simon. "It's still pouring."

"Oh no," Nellie said. "We were going to ride today."

Dawn took a deep breath. No horses to-day. No riding. Great.

She stood up and looked through her suitcase.

Her raincoat was there, but no boots.

She remembered they were home . . . under her bed.

She reached for her sneakers.

Then she saw something yellow flash by.

It was Lizzie Lee in a raincoat.

"Where are you going?" Dawn asked.

Lizzie didn't answer. She raced out the door.

A moment later, Dawn raced out too.

She knew just where Lizzie Lee was going. Straight for the barn.

Outside Dawn could hardly see.

The rain was coming down hard.

It was in her face, in her eyes.

Her hair was soaked.

She dashed into the barn.

"Following me again?" Lizzie was grinning.

Dawn made a face.

It was a friendly one, though.

She looked up . . . up over Woodie.

A picture was tacked to the side of the wall. It was high, easy to miss.

Dawn crossed her fingers. Maybe Lizzie wouldn't spot it.

"Hey." Lizzie pointed.

Dawn stared up at the picture.

It was a woman.

She was wearing a red skirt with ruffles.

A big hoop earring hung from one ear.

"It looks like a—" Dawn said. She covered her mouth. She didn't want to give any clues away.

"A lady pirate," Lizzie said. Then she covered her mouth too.

In back of them the barn door opened. It was Tex.

"Good work," he said. "You found the clue."

"Thanks," said Lizzie.

Dawn narrowed her eyes. "I thought of it last night."

Lizzie laughed. "Me too."

Outside there were voices. Dawn looked out the door.

Everyone was coming.

Miss Perry was first. She was wearing a yellow raincoat. She was carrying a paper bag.

Then came the rest of the campers.

Some of them had raincoats.

Some had umbrellas. The umbrellas were bumping into each other.

Last came Jill Simon. Water was streaming down her Western hat.

"Whew," said Miss Perry. "It's good to get inside."

She pulled off her rain hat. She opened the bag. "Toast and oranges. You two forgot breakfast."

Miss Perry turned to Tex. "It's too wet to ride. We'll help in the barn instead."

Tex handed Dawn a broom.

He gave Lizzie a pail. "Maybe you could get some water. Horses drink a lot."

Dawn stuffed most of the toast in her mouth.

She put the orange in her pocket.

She raced across the front of the barn with the broom.

She wanted Tex to know she was a good worker.

Lizzie was working fast too.

She was running up and down with water for the horses.

Jill worked slower. She was piling hay up in the corner.

Hay was in her hat and in her braids. It was all over her shirt.

She slid down on the pile. "I have the best job," she said.

Dawn swept down the aisle.

The horses were poking their heads out of their stalls. They were watching her.

Blackie showed his teeth.

Dawn raced the broom in the other direction.

The end stall was empty.

There was just a pile of hay and a blanket on a hook.

Dawn looked more closely.

Then she turned around.

Lizzie Lee was carrying water at the other end of the barn.

Good.

Dawn tiptoed into the stall.
She had to get a good look at something.
Something important.
On the blanket was a picture.
It was the same as the clue.
A lady pirate.

···CHAPTER SEVEN···

"Will you carry the sandwiches?" Miss Perry asked Dawn. She looked around. "Maybe Jill can take the drinks."

Dawn put her book under her arm.

She reached for the bag.

Everyone had something to carry.

The campers from Cobra Cabin were going on a picnic.

It was a reading picnic.

Dawn had never heard of that before. But Miss Perry said it was a great day for it. It was sunny and not too hot.

45

Dawn had worried all morning. She thought they'd have to go to the barn.

But today Tex was busy . . . too busy to help them ride.

The campers started to march.

"Are you sure there aren't any mosquitoes?" Lizzie asked. "Or any of those creepy, crawly things?"

Miss Perry laughed. "Don't worry."

They walked along a dirt road.

Then they crossed a field and stopped at a bridge.

For a while they watched the water below. It bubbled along, over the rocks, and into little pools.

Miss Perry pointed to a shady spot across the way.

"Right there," she said. "It's cool under the trees."

The campers spread out blankets.

Dawn looked at the sandwiches.

It was hard to tell what they were. Tuna fish maybe, or chicken salad.

She fished through.

At the bottom was a peanut butter sandwich.

She kept that for herself.

She gave the rest away.

At the same time, Jill was giving out the drinks. "Old G.J.," she said. "Garbage juice."

"Oh no," said Dawn.

"Oh no," said Miss Perry too. She sat back against a tree. She put her glasses on her nose. She opened her book. "This is the life," she said.

Jill pushed her hat back. "I think I'll walk on the rocks."

Miss Perry nodded. She started to read.

Dawn started to read too.

Her book was terrible, though.

It was a mystery, a mystery about a dog and a cat.

Miss Perry had lent it to her. "Daisy Perry," it said on the inside cover.

Dawn had read it before.

She knew what happened in the end.

She took a bite of her sandwich.

Maybe she should walk on the rocks with Jill.

She looked over at Lizzie. Lizzie's book looked good. It had a girl on the cover.

She was wearing long earrings and a frilly skirt.

Dawn leaned over a little. The name of the book was *Barbara the Ballerina*.

Lizzie Lee was sounding out the words.

Dawn lay back. She looked up at the sky.

One of the clouds looked like an angel. Another looked like a horse.

Dawn closed her eyes.

She didn't want to think about horses . . . especially big ones with lots of teeth.

Next to her, Lizzie was laughing. "This book is a riot," she said. "It's about a girl who wants to dance. She keeps making mistakes."

Dawn nodded. "Lend it to me when you're finished."

She stood up. She started toward the water.

Then she stopped.

She thought about the first clue. The pirate lady in the picture.

Then she thought about the one in the horse stall.

It wasn't a pirate at all.

It was a dancing girl.

She scrambled back to the blanket.

Where was her treasure paper?

50

She slapped at her pockets.

Not there.

She turned her book upside down.

The paper fluttered out.

Lizzie looked up from her book. "What's going on?"

Dawn shook her head. She tried not to smile.

Here was one clue that Lizzie didn't know about.

Dawn walked slowly to the water. She held the paper in her hand. She read past the clue about the trail. She'd think about that part later.

The next clue said:

> Look sharp and quick.
> Use both your eyes.
> The dancer is gone,
> and she's hiding our prize.

Dawn closed her eyes.

She tried to think.

Why was there a picture of a dancer in the horse stall?

Who was the dancer?

What prize had she stolen?

There was something else too. It was something about Miss Perry's book.

Dawn put one foot in the water.

A tiny fish came close. It bumped into her toe.

Dawn smiled and wiggled her foot a little.

Yes. She had a feeling Miss Perry's book was important.

If only she knew why.

···CHAPTER EIGHT···

"It's a perfect day to ride," said Miss Perry.

Jill Simon reached for her Western hat.

"Ya-hoo," yelled Nellie.

Dawn sighed. If only it had rained today.

"Maybe I should stay here," she told Miss Perry. "I could work on the mystery."

Miss Perry shook her head. "I don't want you to miss the fun."

"Right." Dawn swallowed.

"Which horse do you want?" Lizzie asked her.

Dawn tried to think.

She remembered Flash.

Flash was always half asleep.

He was so old, he probably didn't have any teeth.

"I'll bet she wants Blackie," said Jill. "He's the tough-looking one."

Dawn swallowed. "I guess I'll take Flash."

"Flash?" said Jill.

"Flash?" said Lizzie.

Dawn crossed her fingers. "I feel sorry for him. No one else wants him."

Lizzie looked at her. "Are you afraid?"

"I'm not afraid of anything," Dawn said. "I'm the Polka Dot Private Eye."

"Me neither," said Lizzie Lee. "I'll take Blackie."

Tex was waiting in front of the barn.

The horses were waiting too.

"Today we'll walk in a circle," said Tex.

"Can I have Blackie?" Lizzie asked.

"Sure," Tex said. He helped her up on Blackie.

Miss Perry helped Jill.

Nellie climbed up by herself.

Dawn took a breath.

She looked at Flash.

Flash opened one eye.

He looked at her.

Then he closed his eye again.

Tex came over. "Let me help you up," he said.

"Poor Flash," said Dawn. "I think he's tired."

"That horse is always tired," said Tex. "He likes to nap."

"Maybe I'll stand here with him." Dawn thought about giving the horse a pat.

She reached up.

Flash turned around to look at her.

She pulled her hand back.

"Just walk him around the circle," Tex said. "Hold on to the reins."

Dawn took the reins slowly.

Tex smiled at her. "Tomorrow we'll ride one of the trails. It'll be different then. Flash loves to do that."

Dawn gulped. She walked to one side of Flash. She didn't want him to step on her.

Next to her, Lizzie was sitting high up on Blackie. "I can't wait to ride a trail," she told Tex. "Which one will it be?"

Tex looked up in the air. "Meadow Walk, I guess." He turned to Miss Perry. "What do you think, Daisy?"

Miss Perry nodded. "Good."

"Daisy?" Jill asked.

Miss Perry grinned. "Just like Donald Duck's girlfriend."

Dawn stopped walking. Daisy.

"Hey," Lizzie said. She was frowning. "Daisy."

Dawn thought hard. That's why the book was important. It had the name Daisy inside.

She thought about the treasure sheet. *Take the right trail . . . the one for Donald and me.*

Donald Duck. Donald and Daisy.

She tried to remember the trails she had seen. There was that funny one . . . Mouse House. Then there was Stone Trail.

She squeezed her eyes tight.

Duck Pond Trail.

Of course. Donald Duck and Daisy would take Duck Pond Trail.

Lizzie's head was turned to one side.

Dawn could see she was trying to figure it out.

She crossed her fingers.

She had to get to Duck Pond Trail before Lizzie Lee. She'd go as soon as she could.

···CHAPTER NINE···

Dawn slapped on her Polka Dot Private Eye hat.

Out of the corner of her eye she could see Lizzie.

Lizzie was spraying Bug-A-Way over the top of her head.

Dawn ducked out of Cobra Cabin first.

She went past the barn . . . toward the trails.

She looked back.

Lizzie was coming out the cabin door.

She was wearing boots and gloves.

She had a net over her Cool Cat hat.

Dawn ran fast.

Branches scratched her arm.

Roots pulled at her feet.

Mosquitoes were flying all over the place.

At last she reached the butterfly tree.

At least she thought it was the butterfly tree.

In back of her, Lizzie was crashing through the leaves.

"Yeow," she yelled.

Mosquitoes, thought Dawn.

Then she stopped.

Lizzie was afraid.

Afraid of bugs.

That's why she was yelling.

That's why she was wearing all that stuff.

Some detective. Afraid of a tiny little . . .

Dawn took a couple of steps.

She thought about Flash . . . and Blackie . . . and being afraid.

She took one more step. Then she sighed.

She cupped her hands around her mouth. "I'll wait for you, Lizzie," she yelled.

A moment later Lizzie appeared. "I'm not afraid," she said. "Not one bit."

Dawn grinned. "I'm not afraid of horses either."

Lizzie opened her mouth. "You are so—" she began. Then she shut her mouth. She grinned too.

They went down the path and turned onto Duck Pond Trail.

The trail was wide and even.

The trees were spread apart.

"What do we look for?" asked Lizzie.

Dawn raised one shoulder. "Who knows?"

In front of them the road stopped.

A white fence ran around a field.

"Hey," yelled Dawn.

A picture of the dancer was painted on the fence.

There was another picture too.

One with a smaller dancer.

"Look," said Lizzie.

They scrambled to the top of the fence.

"I think that's the treasure," Lizzie said.

"You're right," said Dawn. "Absolutely right."

···CHAPTER TEN···

Everyone was in the Devil's Den Dining Room.

It was time for the treasure party.

Dawn stuffed some peanuts in her mouth.

She took a sip of soda.

"Are you sure you don't want garbage juice?" Miss Perry asked.

Dawn smiled. "I'm not afraid of horses anymore," she said as soon as she could talk. "I'm really not."

Lizzie nodded.

"All because of the treasure," said Dawn. "The most beautiful . . . wonderful . . ."

"How did you figure the whole thing out?" Jill said.

Dawn looked at Lizzie.

Lizzie's mouth was filled with potato chips.

They both tried to talk at once.

"We took Duck Pond Trail," said Lizzie. "And then we saw the Dancer in the field."

"Dancer is the name of the horse," said Dawn.

"The mother horse," said Lizzie.

"And the baby—" Dawn began.

"We call the baby a colt," said Tex.

Dawn nodded. "The colt was the treasure."

"Beautiful," said Lizzie, "with a star on his forehead."

Miss Perry came by with a plate of cookies. She put one in Dawn's mouth. "Great detective work, girls," she said.

"Is there a prize?" Jill asked.

Miss Perry smiled. She put the plate of

cookies on the table. "The real prize—" she began.

"Is figuring the whole thing out," said Jill.

Dawn nodded. "That's true."

There was another prize, she thought. She had patted the colt. She had even rubbed the mother's long, smooth side. She had stopped being afraid.

"The real prize," Lizzie said now, "is that I'm not afraid of creepy, crawly things."

"Really?" Jill asked.

Lizzie crossed her fingers. "Almost."

"The real prize," Miss Perry began again, "is that the winners get to name the colt."

Lizzie and Dawn looked at each other.

"Brownie?" asked Lizzie.

"Yucks," said Jill.

"Star?" asked Dawn.

"A little better," said Nellie.

"Think hard," said Miss Perry.

Dawn and Lizzie looked at each other. "I know," said Dawn.

Lizzie nodded. "Me too."

"Treasure," they said together.

"Best name I ever heard," said Miss Perry.

"Me too," said Jill.

Dawn finished the last of her cookie.

She stood up.

"I'm going to the barn with Tex," she told Miss Perry. "It's time for me to ride a horse. A real horse."

Miss Perry smiled. "Go ahead. You might even find another mystery."

Dawn grinned. "I hope so."